Grolier Books

Produced by The Creative Spark
San Clemente, California

Illustrated by Yakovetic Productions

Printed in the United States of America.

ISBN 0-7172-8391-7

Whistles
And Doubloons

Sebastian the crab needed just one more shot to beat Scales at tiddlywinks—for the fifth time that day! "I can make this one with my eyes closed," the confident crab said. Scales watched in amazement as a shiny gold doubloon sailed through the air. It glistened and sparkled in the bright sun, landing with a satisfying "PLONK!" in the coconut shell across the lagoon.

"That's it!" laughed Sebastian. "I win again!"
"Give me another chance, please?" Scales begged. "I know I can beat you this time!"
"Well, okay," Sebastian agreed. "But just one more game."

There was nothing Scales liked better than playing tiddlywinks. Unfortunately, he wasn't very good at it. His first shot skittered across the sand and rolled into the water. "Darn," the disappointed dragon said. "Can I try again?"

His second shot wasn't much better. It flew straight into the air, then landed right back at his feet. "Wait!" he cried. "That doesn't count! I get one more try!"

Scales took a deep breath. He pressed down on the doubloon with all his might. It shot out like a rocket, bounced off a coconut tree, zoomed through the air…

...and smacked Scuttle the seagull right in the head!

"Ow!" yelped the bird as he landed on the island. "That smarts!"

"I'm sorry, Scuttle," Scales apologized. "I didn't mean to hit you. I was trying to get the doubloon into that cup over there. Sebastian and I were playing tiddlywinks and I—"

"Tiddlywinks!" Scuttle exclaimed, interrupting the dragon. "Well, why didn't you say so? I'm the best tiddlywinker anywhere!"

"Do you think you could teach me?" Scales asked. "The tournament is next week and I'd really like to play."

"Well, of course I can!" the boastful bird replied. "I can teach anybody to do anything!"

The next day, Scuttle showed Scales some of his special trick
tiddlywinks shots. There was the Double-Breasted Wing Slapper, the
Alley-Oop, and Scuttle's favorite shot, the Over-And-Under Oompah
Deluxe. "I learned that one from an ostrich," he explained.

But no matter how many times he tried, Scales still couldn't get the hang of it. His first shot landed in a tidepool. His second just missed Scuttle by a feather.

"Not at me, in the coconut!" Scuttle cried, letting out an exasperated whistle.

"What was that wonderful noise you just made?" Ariel asked the bird.

"You mean this?" Scuttle said as he whistled again. "Why, that's whistling, of course. Don't you know how to whistle?"

"No, I don't," the Little Mermaid replied. "I've never even heard of it."

"Oh, it's easy," Scuttle told her. "Just put your lips together and blow."

Ariel gave it a try, but all that came out was a sputter and a little hiss. Even Scales knew how to whistle, but not Ariel.

"Please, Scuttle," she pleaded, "teach me how to whistle!"

"But you promised to teach me how to play tiddlywinks in time for the tournament," whined Scales.

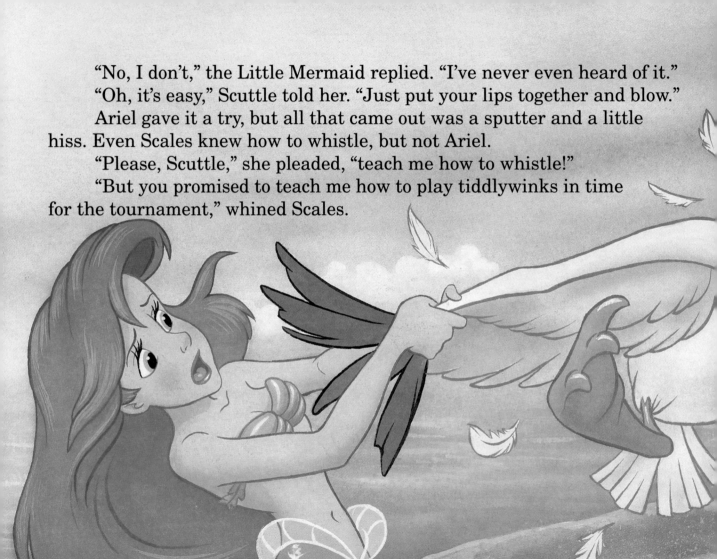

The poor bird had an idea. "I know," he said. "I'll show Scales how to play tiddlywinks during the day, and I'll teach Ariel how to whistle at night!"

By the end of the week, Scuttle the teacher was exhausted. His tail feathers dragged in the sand behind him, and he could barely keep his eyes open. The tournament was only two days away, but Scales still couldn't shoot a doubloon into the shell. And Ariel still hadn't learned how to whistle.

"Keep trying," Scuttle yawned. "Just keep trying."

"Poor Scuttle," Ariel said to Scales. "He must be beat."

"Maybe we should take a break, Scuttle," Scales said. "You look like you could use a nap."

"A nap? I don't need a—" But Scuttle never finished his sentence. He was already fast asleep.

"Come on," Ariel whispered to Scales, "we can practice somewhere else."

When Scuttle awoke from his nap, Ariel and Scales were gone. Scuttle couldn't find them anywhere, but he did find Sebastian. "So," the crusty crustacean said after Scuttle told him what had happened, "I guess teaching is a little harder than you thought, hmm?"

"Teaching is a *lot* harder than I thought!" agreed Scuttle.

"Perhaps some inspiration would help," Sebastian suggested. "Why don't you show Scales the tiddlywinks trophy? He might try harder."

"That's a great idea!" exclaimed Scuttle.

Scuttle grabbed the giant trophy with his feet and took off to find Ariel and Scales, who were practicing by the lagoon. Ariel set a coconut shell at the edge of the shore and encouraged her friend to try again. "You can do it, I know you can!" she said. "Just give it one more try."

"Okay," Scales replied, carefully aiming the doubloon. "Here I go!"
Scales pressed down on the doubloon. It shot straight out, sailing
gracefully through the air and turning end over end until finally...

…it landed right in the shell. "Yay! You did it!" Ariel shouted. And then she let out a long, low whistle without even realizing it. "What was that?" she asked.

"That was you!" Scales told her. "You just whistled!"

"I did?" she said, trying it again. The note came out sweet and clear. "Wow, I really did!"

Just then they saw Scuttle flying overhead—sound asleep! Sebastian's tiddlywinks trophy was dangling from his feet, pulling him toward a thick grove of palm trees.

"Wake up, Scuttle!" Scales cried, but the exhausted bird couldn't hear him.

Just as Scuttle was about to crash, Ariel whistled. The sound startled the seagull and he woke up. "Yeow!" he howled, flapping his wings furiously. "That was close! It's a good thing you whistled just then—hey, wait a minute —you whistled!"

"Isn't it great?" Ariel beamed. "You were right, Scuttle. All I needed to do was keep trying."

"And I know how to shoot now, too," Scales said. "Just wait until you see me at the tournament tomorrow. That trophy is as good as mine."

"How about that!" said Scuttle. "I guess I'm a better teacher than I thought!"

The next day at the tiddlywinks tournament, Scales won
every game. Sebastian watched in amazement as a
shiny gold doubloon sailed through the air. It
glistened and sparkled in the bright sun,
landing with a satisfying "PLONK!" in
the coconut shell across the lagoon.

"Please, Scales," Sebastian pleaded. "Give me another chance. I know I can beat you this time!"

"Well, okay," the dragon said proudly. "But just one more game."